CH
POW

Famous
with **Smokey**

JOE

ALAN MARKS

For Peter and Pauline Mumford
Prowesse and Courtesie

Contents

Goggles

What Zac liked best were the goggles. They had metal frames, yellow-tinted glass and elastic to hold them in place. Zac wanted to wear them propped on his forehead the way Smokey Joe did.

Of course, once sparks began to fly Smokey Joe pulled the goggles over his face straight away. 'Burn your eyes to a cinder otherwise,' he said. And he crouched so closely over the carborundum stone, Zac was worried he'd set his beard on fire.

Fat chance. By now, probably, most of the old man was flame-resistant – not to mention wind- and rain-resistant. Judging by his face and hands (which were all Zac could see) his skin was as gnarled and tough as the bark of an ancient tree. Even his voice had a weather-worn, timbery creak to it if you listened hard.

There was nothing creaky about his fingers,

though. These clamped whatever he was holding like a vice – turning its blade against the buzz of the stone so carefully it was as if a hair's breadth made all the difference.

A hair's breadth?

'Get real,' Zac sniffed. 'This is a knife-grinder you're talking about not a brain surgeon.'

But he went on watching, fascinated.

Afterwards, the goggles back on his forehead, Smokey Joe finished the job with a whetstone for something small (like scissors) or an oilstone for something big (like a chisel). 'Choose your stone carefully, son,' he advised. 'That's important so don't forget it.'

Zac had to smile at this. How could he forget anything to do with Smokey Joe? Smokey Joe was excellent: not a drop-out or a drunk or a derelict like so many sad people back in the city, yet still marvellously, brilliantly free from all the fusspot aspects of life.

Something else was special, too. Smokey Joe made his living with a skill they don't teach in school.

For Zac this made it perfect.

He was up to here – no, *here* – with school. You spent half your time there swotting and the other half trying to guess what was in the teacher's head. Add all the extra work at home and no wonder your brain felt muscle-bound. Besides, where did it get you in the end? After what had happened last week, Zac longed for a plunger he could press down with both hands (the way they do in cartoon films on television) and blow every school in the land to smithereens.

Luckily, drastic action like that wasn't necessary – not now, with this huge, scruffy old man so keen to teach him the tricks of the trade. 'It'll be a fresh start,' Zac told himself. 'There's no such thing as a school for knife-grinders, I bet. All a knife-grinder needs is practice – plus a bit of basic equipment like goggles with yellow-tinted glass.'

No wonder Smokey Joe had him hooked from the moment they met.

The Boneshaker

Breakfast-time it had been, on Zac's very first day in the country.

Birds chirrupped outside, the back door stood wide open and everything on the kitchen table looked so fresh and bright in the Spring sunshine Zac was scared to touch any of it in case he did something wrong. After all, this was a vicarage — with the Reverend and Mrs Reverend sitting opposite, sussing him. Weren't they bound to be a bit posh about mealtimes compared with Jeff and Elsa back at the Children's Home?

Glumly, Zac stared at his boiled egg. Should you bash it with your spoon or zap it with your knife? 'Here,' said Mrs Reverend with a smile. 'Try these, Zac.' She pushed something across the tablecloth — a torture instrument from the look of it. It had fingerholes just like scissors, but instead of blades it was shaped like an oval ring with a set of tiny spikes all round the inside. Was it some kind of thumbscrew, Zac wondered?

The Reverend coughed. 'They've gone a bit blunt, Zac, I'm afraid. Probably you'd do better to – ' Suddenly he stopped. A shadow had fallen across the room as if the sky had clouded over.

Smokey Joe had arrived.

He looked so big in the doorway it was hard to see how he'd squeezed himself through. Almost all of him was covered by a grubby, ankle-length waterproof with slits for his arms and a hole for his head. Everything else was invisible apart from the old-fashioned goggles on his forehead which bunched his shaggy, salt-and-pepper hair into a kind of plume. 'Greetings, your Holiness,' he wheezed. 'Any sharpenin' today for old Joe?'

'Only these,' laughed the vicar. 'Are a pair of egg-cutters worth your while, Joe?'

'If they're worth it to you then they're worth it to me, your Holiness. How about you, young Master. Anythin' you've got that calls for a cuttin' edge?'

'Me?' Zac blinked in alarm.

'This is Zac,' the vicar explained. 'He's here from the city for a holiday. Zac, meet Smokey Joe – who's pretty well-known in these parts.

11

So is his splendid bicycle!'

'Bicycle?' said Zac.

'Want to see it, son?' Smokey Joe asked.

Zac could tell at once what an honour this was. The Reverend and Mrs Reverend beamed at each other and hovered politely on the back step as the enormous, shambling old man led him along the garden path, under the yew trees and out into the lane behind the house.

The bike itself stopped Zac in his tracks. 'There she is, me ol' beauty,' said Smokey Joe.

'Er . . . custom-built, is it?' Zac asked, cautiously.

'Custom-built?' Smokey Joe gave a snort at such city-speak. 'Got no opinion on custom-built, son. Custom-built is neither hither nor youn to my way of thinkin'. What counts is . . . this boneshaker suits me. Every nut and bolt of it *suits* me. See that, can you?'

'Yes,' said Zac. Actually, he couldn't see it at all.

For a start the bike had no tyres. Its wheels were nothing but rims pitted with rust. Nor was there a saddle, strictly speaking, since the place where this should have been was covered by a long, wooden toolbox lashed to the bike's main frame.

How were you supposed to ride the thing?

At least it had handlebars, Zac noticed. These were almost normal – compared with the front of the vehicle, anyway. For here, mounted in a cast-iron basket, was the real business of the bike: a twelve-volt car battery, with fanbelt attachment, linked to a six-inch grindstone. 'What's that?' Zac asked, as something else caught his eye.

'It's called an umbrella, son. Don't you have umbrellas in the city?'

'Yes, but what's it *for*?'

Smokey Joe stared at him. Then he fumbled beneath the flaps where the fixing was and opened the umbrella over the basket like a great, circular bat. 'Keeps the rain off when I'm workin',' he said.

Zac felt like a right wally. 'Er . . . what I meant was, you go out in all weathers, do you?'

'Right round the clock and right through the calendar, as well. Can't let a drop of cloud-juice put me off. Or snow, come to that. A royal pain in the backside, snow is. And storms is even worse . . . got meself struck by lightnin' once, y'know. That's why they call me Smokey.' He chuckled as if this were a joke.

By now Zac was ready to believe anything. Especially after Joe had wired up the battery, pulled down the goggles and begun dab-dab-

dabbing with the egg-cutters while the grindstone span and span. Tiny sparks sprinkled his hands.

Zac could have watched forever.

Soon, though, Joe straightened up. He tested the spikes with his thumb. 'Sharp as a kitten's claws,' he pronounced. 'You could snip the top off a billiard ball now – never mind a boiled egg.'

But he wasn't finished yet. From the toolbox, he took a whetstone no bigger than a nail-file. This, with the gentlest of strokes, he rubbed over each point in turn. 'Never, never rush yourself,' he told Zac. 'Small jobs or big jobs – treat 'em both with respect.'

'Right,' said Zac.

Smokey Joe gave him a sideways look. 'What's your line of work, son?' he asked.

'Me?' Zac said bitterly. 'I'm still at school.'

'At your age?'

'All eleven-year-olds are. If they're not it's against the law.'

'That a fact?' Smokey Joe shook his head in despair at this waste of a nation's eleven-year-olds. 'Carborundum,' he said.

'Sorry?'

'This grindstone here. Carborundum, it is. The very best. Nothin' else will do, son. Bear that in mind, eh? You can pass it on to the other kids when you get back to the classroom.'

'Carborundum,' Zac said. 'Carborundum.' He rolled the word over his tongue: carborundum, carborundum, carborundum – like the motto on a coat-of-arms.

Zac fancied a coat-of-arms.

His would show yellow-tinted goggles on a field of flying sparks with the words ZAC CARBORUNDUM EST underneath – meaning, ZAC IS THE SHARPEST. Something like that, anyway. Of course, a kid from a Children's Home with a coat-of-arms was bound to be a bit odd. As odd as Smokey Joe, even.

Suddenly, in his thin, wheedly voice, the old man spoke again. 'So it's a holiday you're on,' he said. 'A holiday with his Holiness . . .'

'That's right.'

'How are you fixed for time, then? All booked up, are you? With trips and treats and suchlike?'

Zac shrugged. 'I don't really know. I only got here last night.'

'Last night, eh?' Smokey Joe nodded thoughtfully as if this were the worst possible time for anyone to arrive anywhere. He gave a loud, gurgling sniff. 'Got plenty of jobs lined up for meself over the weekend, y'see – some big and some small but all of 'em needin' respect.

Any chance you could tag along and give me a hand?'

'Me?'

'Well, it's you I'm lookin' at.'

Zac couldn't believe his ears. 'I'd . . . I'd have to check with the Reverend,' he said. 'And with Mrs Reverend.'

'You do that, son. Bein' Sunday an' all, you'll be bobbin' and weavin' in church this mornin', I shouldn't wonder. No church this afternoon, though. So the knock on the door you'll hear first thing after dinner will be me come for your answer. Cheery-bye, then.'

'Cheery-bye,' Zac replied. He stood in the lane, staring, long after Smokey Joe and his well-known bicycle had disappeared.

Already, though, carrying the egg-cutters back indoors as carefully as if they were made of glass, he felt the first pangs of disappointment. After all, was it even worth mentioning the old man's invitation to the Reverend and Mrs Reverend?

He knew exactly what Jeff and Elsa would have said.

Getting Permission

His first chance to raise the subject came later that morning, after church. 'Enjoy the Service, Zac?' his Holiness asked.

'Fine,' said Zac.

'Really?' The vicar looked at him in surprise. 'Wasn't it rather . . . well, *wordy* for you?'

'I like words.'

This was true. Some of them still echoed in Zac's head: Venite, Exultemus Domino . . . Benedicte Omnia Opera . . . Jubilate Deo. They sounded nearly as good as ZAC CARBORUNDUM EST.

Of course, he wasn't sure what they meant because primary school kids don't do proper Latin. Something else puzzled him, too. 'Why do you sing them in that funny voice?' he asked. 'Why not just say them?'

The vicar laughed. 'It's a kind of dressing-up, I suppose, to make church-going seem a bit special. Like this long white gown I wear and this scarf-thing round my neck.'

'Vestments,' Zac said.

'You do like words, don't you,' said the vicar. He eyed Zac warily as if he'd been told too little about him . . . or maybe too much.

Anyway, who cared what the Reverend thought? Smokey Joe's opinion was the important one. Quickly, Zac glanced round the church.

It was empty now apart from the two of them. Sunlight, filtering through the stained-glass windows, splashed crooked puddles of colour across the flagstones and smooth wooden pews and glinted so brightly on the brasswork it seemed to be solid gold. He took a deep breath. 'Er . . . Reverend?' he said.

'Yes?' The vicar smiled encouragingly.

Instantly Zac lost his nerve. 'That . . . that window over there,' he pointed. 'D'you reckon it's the sort of thing you should have in a church?'

'Ah,' said the vicar. 'Well spotted, Zac. Plenty of people would agree with you there. More like a page from a picture book, they say – or even a comic.'

'Is it St George?' Zac asked.

'That's the general opinion. But some

19

scholars suggest it's a portrait of King Arthur himself. What do you think?'

Zac had spent most of the vicar's sermon pondering this very question but he still hadn't made up his mind.

He stared at the window.

There was no mystery about the dragon, of course. What else could it be, so coiled and knobbly, with its snake-like eyes and fiery snout scorching the air all round it? The man in armour was more of a problem. His sword was poised to come slicing downwards but whether this was Saintly or Royal depended on how you looked at it. Besides, with no sign of a motto or coat-of-arms for identification, how could anyone decide for sure? 'It's St George,' said Zac eventually.

'Why?'

'Because otherwise it wouldn't be here.'

The vicar nodded. 'That's the safe conclusion, Zac. Church-goers usually settle for what's safe, I'm afraid. Pity, really. St George was a fine fellow, no doubt about that . . . but King Arthur would be much more fun.' He peered over his spectacles. 'Do you know what's always puzzled me ever since I was a lad? When they're wearing all that clobber, which must be like clanking around inside a set of joined-up dustbins, how

20

on earth do they go to the loo?'

'Yeah,' Zac agreed. 'It must be bad enough wearing vestments.'

'At least those can't get rusty,' the vicar chuckled.

'Not much use against a dragon, though.'

'That's true.'

By now the vicar had finished lining up the hymn-books for the evening service and was fumbling in his pocket for the keys to the church door. 'It's a triple lock,' he explained. 'You can't be too careful about thieves these days – even deep in the country like this.'

'What would they steal?' Zac asked.

'Oh . . . things.' He looked uncomfortable as if he didn't want to specify what things exactly.

'Hey,' said Zac. 'You don't think *I'd* steal them, do you?'

'What? No . . . no, of course not.'

Zac could tell he was lying. He scowled.

The Reverend must have known from the start that this wasn't a holiday so much as a cooling-off period – that Zac had been sent here to clear the air back at the Children's Home after last week's calamity.

He felt the vicar's hand on his arm. 'Zac, are you all right?'

'Brilliant,' Zac said.

'Not worried about something? Something you and I could talk over, perhaps?'

'Like what?' said Zac, pulling away.

They were out on the front path now. Overhead, the churchyard trees shifted their branches moodily as if the breeze wasn't doing them any favours, thank you, so don't expect any favours back.

Zac knew the feeling.

So why not just trust his luck? 'Hey,' he called over his shoulder. 'Is it all right with you if I tag along with Smokey Joe this afternoon? He's asked me to give him a hand.'

'Smokey Joe did?' said the vicar in surprise.

22

'Smokey Joe actually asked you to help him?'

'Sure,' said Zac. 'He'll be knocking on your door after dinner to see if it's okay.'

'And is it okay?'

'What?'

'Is it okay?' the vicar repeated.

Zac swung round. 'You're asking *me*?'

'Well, it's your holiday, Zac. I'm sure we can come up with a suitable excuse if you'd rather say no – you've only just met him, after all. And he is, to put it mildly, a little out of the ordinary. Mind you, there are plenty of youngsters round here who'd jump at the chance to be Smokey Joe's assistant. As I mentioned at breakfast, he's something of a local hero!'

'So you'll actually let me?' Zac blinked.

'Let you?'

'Go with him, I mean – him being an old man and me just a kid an' that.'

The vicar stared at him, baffled. Then, as he understood, he looked shocked. 'Zac,' he protested. 'This is Smokey Joe we're talking about!'

'I know,' said Zac hastily, 'I know. I promise I'll look after him properly.'

'You'd better!' The look on his Holiness's face was as stern as Saint George's, or maybe King Arthur's, in the stained-glass window.

Even his voice sounded dressed-up again.

He glowered down at Zac. 'Believe me, young man, Smokey Joe *matters* to the people round here. Let that old fellow down and you'll have the whole county after your blood. So don't accept his invitation unless you're prepared to back him up one hundred per cent. Is that clear?'

'Okay,' said Zac, 'okay. No need to bang on about it, Reverend. I reckon I've got the message.' Also, he'd got exactly what he wanted.

Maybe that's what was so scary all of a sudden.

A Good Doss For Ghosts

'Really?' Zac asked, still not believing it. 'Once upon a time you were struck by lightning, Joe?'

'Frazzled,' said Smokey Joe. 'Done to a crisp, I was – like a sausage left in a fryin' pan.' He grinned toothily, his shoulders bib-bobbing up and down and his breath coming in little hisses and snorts. Zac wondered what was so funny. He thought of the telegraph pole outside the Children's Home which an electric storm had left split and smouldering . . . unless Smokey Joe was teasing again. Quite a lot of the time he seemed to be teasing.

This cut-down waterproof, for instance.

Was that a tease? Zac examined it, doubtfully. It rustled and flapped round his ankles as he walked. 'Do I *have* to wear this?' he complained.

'Dogs,' Smokey Joe said.

'What?'

'Dogs, son. The bane of my life they are – all barks and bites and dollops for you to tread in. Dogs is diabolical in my opinion. That there cape I've given you fools 'em, though. Bein' so loose an' all it gives 'em somethin' to snap at that isn't you – and isn't too tasty, neither. See these holes? Mouths they came from, not moths.'

Zac stared at the perforations in Smokey Joe's waterproof. His mini-version didn't seem such a bad idea after all. Besides, it made him look more like Smokey Joe, didn't it?

Except, of course, when he was in charge of the bike.

Zac still hadn't got the hang of the bike. All its weight was at the front, that was the trouble, so the whole contraption was liable to tip over in a jangling heap when he tried to bring it to a halt. Another problem was propping it upright for an actual job. Twice Zac had bungled this and finished flat on his back with the bike on top of him. The shame of it still made him go hot and cold. Not that Smokey Joe seemed to mind very much. He'd simply clucked his tongue as if it were no more than he expected from an eleven-year-old who'd been forced to waste so many years in school.

School?

Zac shook his head in wonder. Already school seemed a million miles away and a million years ago. And that was exactly where he wanted it — so if Jeff and Elsa thought otherwise, tough luck.

Suddenly, Smokey Joe lifted a hand. 'Whoa back, son,' the old man said. 'Here's a regular customer.'

'This place?'

'Grand, in't it,' said Smokey Joe.

That was just the word, Zac felt.

The gateway in the long flint wall they'd been following for the last half-hour was impressive enough with its stone pillars on either side and its carving of a lion and a unicorn high on the arch overhead. Looking through the elaborate ironwork of the gate itself, though, Zac was astonished by what lay beyond. 'Is it a palace?' he exclaimed. 'Or some sort of castle, maybe?'

'A bit of both, son, in its time.'

'We're going in, Joe?'

'Why not?'

'Shouldn't . . . shouldn't we be trying the back door, though?'

'This *is* the back door,' Smokey said. The gate clattered shut behind them.

It was like a movie, Zac decided. The sky was a brighter blue here and the grass a deeper green

– as if, somehow, they'd stumbled on-screen at a cinema. Even the outline of towers and turrets ahead of them looked blacker and crisper than they should have done. 'And we're *in* the movie,' Zac whispered. 'This is actually happening . . .' Of course, he was only an extra. Smokey Joe was the star. Wheeling the bike one-handed, his goggles glinting in the sunlight, the old man seemed to know the script by heart.

Which was just as well, Zac felt, in a place as moated and make-believe as this.

Close up, it was more impressive than ever. He stared at the windows all round him in what Smokey Joe called 'the kitchen courtyard'. Did that mean there was a dining-room courtyard, too? Or a courtyard that led off the sitting-room – or sitting-rooms, more like? In a building this size there might even have been a throne-room, for all Zac knew, attached to the most majestic courtyard of all. 'Who lives here?' he asked. 'Some kind of Lord or Lady, is it?'

'Ghosts,' said Smokey Joe.

'Ghosts?'

'Ghosts mostly, yes. Can't you see 'em flittin' back and forth just out of eye-shot, son? This place is full of the things. Not surprisin', neither, considerin' it changes no more than they do. A good doss for ghosts, this is.'

28

'Yeah . . .' said Zac. At the back of his mind he could hear the crunch of high-topped boots and the mutter of words like 'prithee' and 'God's bodkins'.

Smokey Joe gave another of his sniffs. 'Naturally, it's got some flesh-and-blood folk, too.' He nodded towards a doorway that was the shape of a shield upside-down. There, more inside than out, stood a bent, wrinkled old woman in a black dress.

'Who's that?' Zac asked.

'Mrs Reeve, Head of Household,' Smokey said. 'Sixty inches of sourness, she is. Runs this place strict as a sergeant-major. Don't cross her, son. Not ever. That tongue of hers can pickle you in vinegar and serve you up like a walnut. Nasty bit of work, she is. Don't scare me, though.'

'No?'

Smokey Joe gave a chuckle. 'Found out her weakness long ago,' he declared.

'Weakness?' said Zac. 'What's that?'

'She fancies me.'

'What?'

'No need to sound so surprised, son.'

'Sorry,' Zac grinned. His smile faded at once, though, as they got closer and he saw Mrs Reeve was staring at him.

'Who are you, boy?' she snapped. 'What are you doing here?'

'Er . . .'

'Speak up!'

'I'm sharpenin',' said Zac. 'At least, that's what I'm learning to do. Egg-cutters and stuff . . .'

'Egg-cutters?'

'Well, not just egg-cutters . . .'

'I should think *not*.' The old woman glared at him fiercely, her head poking forward on her neck like a tortoise. Over her arm was a basket piled high with carving-knives but she held this tight to her side as if for safe-keeping. 'Is he black, Joe?' she asked suddenly. 'Is it a black boy you've brought here?'

'Now that you mention it, ma'am,' said Smokey Joe, 'I do believe he is.'

'Come here, boy,' the old woman barked. 'Yes, it's you I'm talking to. No need to be shy – I won't bite you.'

'Go on, son,' Smokey Joe prompted.

Zac shuffled forward. 'Closer,' she ordered. 'My eyes aren't what they used to be.' Zac was so close now he could smell the starch in her dress.

She peered up at him, her not-what-they-used-to-be-eyes like flat, brown coins in her

leathery face. She brushed his cheek with a fingertip. 'So Smokey Joe chose you, did he?' she murmured. 'I wonder why?'

'Why not?' said Zac.

'Don't be so huffy, boy. It's a fair question after all these years when Smokey's worked on his own. Those of us who care about the old codger are bound to be curious . . . and bound to be wary, come to that. For instance, you're a handsome lad, I'll admit, but are you good-hearted? And will you be brave enough when the time comes?'

'Brave enough?' said Zac. 'Brave enough for what?'

'You'll see,' said the old woman. She tapped the side of her nose as if this were a deep, dark secret she couldn't possibly share with the likes of him — not yet, anyway.

Zac wanted to kick her.

What stopped him was Smokey Joe's Golden Rule for staying-in-business. 'Take my word for it, Zac,' he'd insisted. 'Stick to this and you'll be spared a lot of hassle: THE CUSTOMERS ARE ALWAYS RIGHT . . . ESPECIALLY WHEN THEY'RE SO FAR WRONG YOU WANT TO THROTTLE 'EM. Bear that in mind, son. It never fails.'

So Zac swallowed the remark on the tip of his

tongue. 'I'll do my best, ma'am,' he said.

'That's a promise?'

'It is, yes.'

'Why?' she demanded.

'Sorry?'

'What's in it for you, boy? All this gallivanting around with old Joe . . . where d'you expect it to get you? Will you end up rich, do you think? Or famous?'

'Famous?' said Zac. 'With Smokey Joe?'

'You'd be surprised,' said the old woman drily. 'There's a lot more to him than that ridiculous mackintosh, you know.'

'I'm wearing one, too,' Zac pointed out.

'So I noticed . . . in which case, you'd better make yourself useful. Here, put this basket where Joe can reach it. And watch what he's doing closely. You may learn something.'

Zac gritted his teeth. 'I have been, ma'am,' he said. 'All afternoon.'

'And he's quick on the uptake as well,' Smokey Joe assured her. 'No flies on this lad, I can – ' He broke off.

Zac had heard it, too.

It came from deep in the castle – from some open-air space like this one, Zac guessed, to judge by the echo. It was a sound that suited the place perfectly except it was at least six

33

centuries out of date. 'Is that . . .?' he began. 'No, it can't be.'

'Can't be?' the old woman sniggered. 'You'd be surprised at what goes on in this house, boy.'

'Yes, but – '

'Want to look for yourself?' She didn't think he'd dare, that was obvious.

'Yeah,' said Zac. 'Why not? That okay with you, Joe?'

'Go ahead, son.'

'Through this door and down the passage,' she directed him. 'Turn left at the far end into the yard directly opposite.'

'Thanks,' said Zac. Not that he needed Mrs Reeve's help. Or any persuading to get away from her, the old bat.

Mind you, as he forced himself step by step along the empty whitewashed corridor with its hooks on either side where weapons had once hung, Zac was much more nervous of the din up ahead than he cared to admit.

Could it possibly be the real thing?

Surely ghosts were out of the question . . . but why should anyone fake so convincingly the slither and clash of sword against sword?

In the Tiltyard

They were armour-clad, both of them: breastplates, greaves, sabatons, helmets with lowered vizors. And the swords they wielded were huge – double-edged and double-handed. Maybe that's why they moved so heavily, in slow motion almost, more like lumberjacks than combatants. 'Who are they?' Zac asked.

'In the white plume, Sir Lancelot,' came the answer. 'In the green and gold, Sir Gawain.' The speaker was sprawled on a bench against the castle wall. He was bare-headed, his helmet cradled in his lap, but otherwise as fully armed as the two fighters. Zac liked the look of his close-cropped hair and designer-stubble . . . also his eyes, green and friendly, despite the strain of staring into the bright, Spring sunshine. 'I'm Zac,' he introduced himself. 'On holiday, sort of, from the city.'

'And I'm Sir Bedevere, would you believe.'

35

'Not really, no.'

'No?' Sir Bedevere pulled a face. 'Listen, Zac, this Camelot kit I'm wearing isn't just snazzy, you know – it's authentic in every detail. So how comes it doesn't fool you?'

'That cigarette in your hand. You shouldn't be smoking.'

'No ashtrays on the round table, huh?'

'No tobacco,' Zac said. 'It wasn't brought to this country till centuries later.'

'Sharp lad,' said Sir Bedevere. He stubbed out the cigarette and patted the bench beside him. 'Take the weight off your feet,' he invited, 'or the lack of weight, I should say, since you're not up to your eyebrows in ironmongery like the rest of us.'

'*Over* your eyebrows,' said Zac. 'When you're wearing that helmet, anyway.'

'Wait till you get a thump on top of it, my friend – the shock travels down your body, through your knees and pretty nearly sprains your ankles. And that's when you're *expecting* it.'

'Is that why they're rehearsing?' Zac asked. 'To make sure they're always expecting it?'

'Bulls-eye, kid. Every move must be planned in advance – though it shouldn't look that way, of course. The trick is to convince the punters

36

we're knocking seven bells out of each other. Sometimes we are, too, if we get one of the sequences wrong.'

'When's the tournament, then?'

'Tomorrow afternoon . . . starts at two o'clock on the dot with a procession down in the village square. It's our last performance before we move up north for the Summer. So if you're anywhere in the vicinity, listen for a fanfare of trumpets.'

'Do you play those as well?'

'You bet we do. Knights-of-all-trades, we are – offering a complete service apart from tearing the tickets and selling the ice-creams. The management takes care of those . . . along with providing a first-aid post, just in case. Over there, see?'

Beyond the tiltyard, through an archway wide enough to frame acres of parkland, Zac saw tents decked with pennants. There were people moving about, too, in medieval costume. At this distance it was anyone's guess whether they were ghosts or flesh and blood.

Sir Bedevere heaved himself clankingly to his feet. 'Here come Sir Lance and Sir Gav in person,' he said. 'Must want a tea-break already, the lazy stiffs.'

'Hi, kid,' Sir Lancelot waved as he approached.

'Or should I be saying "young squire"?'

'Yes, you should,' said Sir Gawain. 'Something else you've forgotten, Lance – along with most of our routines this morning. I've got so many dents in these tin pyjamas of mine I feel like a car that's been through a crusher!'

When they took off their helmets – showing Gawain with lank, fair hair plastered flat to his forehead and Lancelot bald as a nut – both were grinning broadly.

So was Sir Bedevere. 'We're in luck, team,' he told them. 'This is Zac – who's a refugee from the city just like us. He's an expert on the Age of Chivalry.'

'I'm glad somebody is,' said Sir Lancelot. 'What are you doing out here in the boondocks, Zac?'

'I've got a job.'

'A job?'

'I'm working with Smokey Joe. He's a knife-grinder.'

Sir Gawain laughed. 'A knife-grinder, eh? I thought knife-grinders were extinct.'

'I thought knights were.'

'Ouch!' said Sir Bedevere. 'You *are* a sharp kid, Zac. Top of the class in school, I bet.' Zac didn't answer. What could he say to that?

In any case, what business was it of theirs? Some things are private and should stay that way.

He kept his gaze fixed on his feet, terrified he might burst into tears. 'Something wrong, Zac?' said Sir Bedevere gently. 'Did I drop some sort of clanger, there? Always have had a big mouth, I'm afraid.'

'Nothing,' Zac said. 'Nothing's wrong.'

'You're sure?'

'Positive.'

'Well, that's a relief.' It wasn't, though. Embarrassing is what it was.

Gawain pretended to dry his hair while Lancelot fussed with the elbow-joint on his sword-arm. It was Sir Bedevere who smoothed things over. 'Hey,' he exclaimed. 'Want to try out some of our accoutrements, Zac? That's a posh word for armour, by the way.'

'It isn't,' said Zac. 'It means everything *except* your armour.'

'See? I told you this kid was an expert. Gav, your sword, please . . . and Lance, kindly pass me that shield. Now, let's find out if my helmet fits that noddle of yours.' Already he was settling it over Zac's head.

It was heavier than Zac expected and smelt of metal polish and stale sweat. When he lowered the vizor he was surprised at how little he could see – like viewing the world through the grill in a dungeon door.

Who cared about that, though? The shield hung clumsily on his arm and the sword was too tall for him but everything together felt wonderful: ZAC CARBORUNDUM EST.

Sir Lancelot gave a whistle of admiration.

'Sensational, Zac,' he pronounced.

'*Sir* Zac,' Gawain corrected him.

'Yeah,' Zac whispered. '*Sir* Zac.' He imagined a battle and himself in the thick of it. Would he be the winner or the loser?

Suddenly the armour felt hot and heavy, so he laid down the sword and shield and lifted the helmet from his shoulders.

'Had enough already?' said Sir Bedevere. 'Can't say I blame you. In warm weather that helmet's like balancing a micro-wave on your bonce.'

'A bit,' Zac agreed.

'Why not stick around for a while?' Sir Lancelot suggested. 'We'll be fetching the horses soon.'

'Horses?'

'Certainly. We don't just make fools of ourselves on foot, you know. You can also watch us kebab each other with lances at full gallop.'

'Or *not* kebab each other,' Sir Bedevere said. 'Being actors rather than athletes, mostly we miss by a mile.'

'Especially if someone — who'd better be nameless — forgets every move,' said Sir Gawain. 'Or falls off head first. Or ties himself in such a knot he's riding back-to-front,

41

practically. It's a thrill-a-minute on this team.'

'The truth is, we're so new to this game we're a bit out of our depth,' Sir Bedevere admitted. 'What we really need is a technical adviser – someone like you, Zac, come to think of it. Now, there's an idea! What if we hired you to coach us for a couple of days? That's all it would take to smarten us up, I'm sure.'

'How about Smokey Joe?'

'We'll pay him a transfer fee . . . for forty-eight hours of your time. That way everyone comes out smiling. So what's your answer, kid? Is it a deal?'

What could Zac say?

He stared at the three of them, hearing cheers and fanfares in his head.

Then he bit his lip. 'Sorry,' he said. 'It's just that Smokey Joe asked me first. He'll be waiting for me right now, I expect – with the oilstone, probably. Or maybe the whetstone.'

'Fair enough,' said Sir Bedevere. 'Mustn't keep the old oilstone and whetstone waiting.'

'Look,' said Zac, blushing. 'I can get you a special offer if you like. I'll ask Smokey Joe to sharpen all your stuff at half-price. He really will, I promise.'

'*What*?'

'You want us to commit *suicide*?' Sir Lancelot

42

and Sir Gawain were wide-eyed with horror.

'No offence, Zac,' said Sir Bedevere, 'but it's a strict rule of ours to keep our equipment as *un*-sharp as we possibly can. It's the only way to survive in our trade. Could your friend Smokey Joe make it *blunter* by any chance?' Even Zac had to laugh at this.

Soon they were all laughing. It was the right cue for an exit, as Zac was quick to recognise, but at the door into the passageway he hesitated for a moment. 'Probably Smokey Joe and me will be too busy for tomorrow's tournament,' he called. 'But maybe we can get to the village square for the procession.'

'We'll watch out for you, Zac,' said Sir Bedevere. 'Kindly keep that grindstone under control, though.'

'Not to mention the oilstone,' Sir Lancelot winced.

'Or whetstone,' added Sir Gawain.

And there in the sunshine, with timing too perfect to be improved upon for once, they lifted the hilts of their swords to their chins in a slow, knightly salute.

Zac almost saluted back.

He was learning fast.

By now Zac could tell at a glance which jobs would be done at the front door and which would be round at the back. Front-door jobs were usually fun. At the back door it was important to stay serious, though, and show you knew your place. 'Why is that, Joe?' he asked.

Smokey looked up from the kitchen-shears he was mending. 'Some folk just need to look down on you,' he shrugged. 'Seein' you on the level gets 'em all upset. Don't ask me why.'

'So they can't share a joke with you?'

'Only lookin' down,' Smokey said. 'Or if you're lookin' up. It has to be the one or the other.'

'How about if you look down and they look up?'

'Doesn't work, son. I've tried it.'

Zac could see the problem. This lady, for

example, hardly looked at him at all when she handed over her money.

Now there was another thing: the money. 'Why is it always the big houses where they count every penny of their change?' he frowned. 'At the little houses they never seem to bother – they just give it straight back to you as a tip.'

'Not always,' said Smokey Joe. 'Just mostly.'

'Why, though?'

'Arithmetic,' Smokey declared. 'The bigger the house, the worse they are at arithmetic.'

'Really?' said Zac, scratching his head.

'Makes sense, doesn't it?'

'Well . . .'

'There you are, then,' the old man winked.

After this came more lessons in fiddle-faddle (as he called it). Already Zac had got the measure of fiddle-faddle. He could take apart hedge-cutters, dis-assemble a lawn mower, loosen any nut, bolt, catch or fixing he came across . . . and put each of them back together as neatly as if it were new. 'Any edge can be sharpened, son.' Smokey Joe insisted. 'Provided you can get at it properly.'

Here, of course, he was referring to the pincers and pliers and spanners and screwdrivers he kept in the wooden box strapped to his bike. 'Pick the right tool and the job's half finished,' he told Zac over and over again.

Too often, to tell the truth. Zac's head ached nearly as much as his fingers. When Smokey Joe announced that a tea-break was in order because he was 'off to see a man about an oil-can', Zac almost sighed out loud with relief.

As soon as the old man was out of sight, he looked for a place to rest. Over there on the village green, perhaps? He could prop the bike against a tree trunk, fold his waterproof up for a pillow and let himself doze awhile on the grass.

At least, that's what he intended to do but he must have been more worn out than he thought.

He wasn't sure what eventually woke him. Maybe it was a touch of cramp or a sudden chill in the air. Then again, maybe he'd been nudged

by one of the big kids who stood in a circle all round him, staring down from a darkening sky.

Slowly, not making any sudden moves, Zac eased himself into a sitting position. 'Wakey-wakey,' said the biggest kid of all.

She was enormous. And most of her was muscle. Even Zac's first glance told him that. What did they do here in the country – wrestle cows?

He tried to smile.

She didn't bother smiling back. Her leather jacket crackled as she folded her arms. 'You from the city?' she asked.

'That's right.'

'Thought as much. I'm from round here . . . like these mates of mine. They're from round here, too.'

'Fine,' said Zac.

'Fine, is it? Bein' country an' all?'

'Why not?'

Now she did smile but not so he felt any better. One of her front teeth was missing and another, next to the gap, was gold. It glittered as she turned to the others. 'Reckon that must be a compliment,' she said, 'comin' from a city-kid.'

'Yeah,' said the boy to her left. 'A compliment, that is. Does the city-kid mean it, though . . . there's the aggravation. Maybe he's lookin' down his nose at us all along.'

He was her second-in-command, Zac decided, being the closest in size and nastiness. Not that the others were very different. He didn't fancy his chances with any of them. 'Reckon I'll be off, then,' he said, standing up as casually as he could.

'Already?' said the big girl.

'If that's okay with you . . .'

'Course it is, city-kid. You can please yourself what you do in our book. That's providin' you leave the bike behind.'

'The bike?'

'The bike, yes. That funny-looking contraption leanin' against the tree behind you. Belong to you, does it?'

'Sort of.'

'Don't look like no city-kid's bike.'

'I'm . . . I'm taking care of it,' Zac said. 'Till my friend gets back.'

'Till your friend gets back, eh? So it's not actually your bike, then. More *borrowed*, you might say . . .' The big girl nodded knowingly, curling her tongue into the gap where her tooth should have been. The sucking sound as she did it was the most sinister Zac had ever heard.

He tried again. 'Not much use to anyone else,' he said brightly. 'The bike, I mean. It just

48

happens to suit my friend, that's all. I'll tell him you were interested in it, though.'

'Interested in it?' said the big girl. 'Oh, we're interested in it all right. What's more, we'd quite like to meet this friend o' yourn, too. Expected soon, is he?'

'Any minute,' said Zac quickly.

'*That* soon? Now there's lucky. We won't have to hang about, will we . . . and neither will you. In fact, why don't you get goin' like you said and let us do the lookin' after – since your friend'll be back any minute.'

'Well . . .'

'What's this, city-kid? Don't you trust us? Because we trust you, you know. Sure as eggs is eggs we trust you. Let's do a deal, shall we? You leave the bike with us . . . and we'll hand it over to your friend as soon as he comes to collect it. What could be fairer than that?'

'Nothing, I suppose.'

'It's settled, then. Shall we shake on it?'

She held out a hand which reminded Zac of a come-to-life version of the catcher's mitt Jeff and Elsa had brought back from their holiday in America. He wished he were wearing it now. His own hand looked small and pathetic as it reached towards hers. What else could he do, though? 'Okay,' he said.

Her fingers closed over his.

And went on closing.

Zac's gasp of pain was so solid in his throat, he half-expected to see it bounce down to the grass as his mouth fell open. There were grins all round him now with the biggest and gappiest and most glittery only an arm's-length or so away. 'Hey,' he yelped. 'That hurts!'

'Really?' Her grip grew tighter still. 'Not as much as this, I bet,' she hissed.

'No . . .' Zac whimpered.

It was agony. Surely his fingers would be crushed. They'd crumble to dust in her fist. How could he help Smokey Joe one-handed?

That, surely, was what counted . . .

So Zac swivelled, sagged at the knees and backed himself into her — using all her bodyweight as leverage and his own shoulder as a pivot — just the way Jeff had shown him at Judo Club. The split-second as she somersaulted over his head seemed to last forever . . . till, with a bone-jarring, grass-flattening crash she landed on her back between him and the tree. One of her feet caught the bike itself so it tottered a moment, as if to make up its mind, then collapsed clatteringly on top of her.

She lay perfectly still.

Someone coughed uneasily and asked, 'Is our

Jessie dead, then, or what?'

'Nah,' said her second-in-command. 'Just winded.' His eyes were looking Zac over. Suddenly all their eyes were looking Zac over. 'What's your next trick, city-kid?' he asked.

Zac lifted a hand. 'Shake?' he offered.

The sheer cheek of it almost saved him. If the bike had been upright and he'd had the nerve to wheel it away (taking care not to tip it over), probably they'd have been too amazed to stop him.

Real life isn't like that, though. Already they were edging towards him. He couldn't possibly tackle all five, he realised. Jeff's Judo Club wasn't that good. Still, he hadn't done badly so far. He might as well go out in style. So, half-crouching, half on tiptoe, Zac began to twist and turn on the spot — his hands and feet

making sudden stabs in the air like a kung-fu kickboxer.

This almost saved him, too.

He saw them draw back. 'He's vicious, he is,' one of them warned. 'Go for your vitals, he will – or your windpipe.'

'Leave off . . . he's just bluffin'.'

'You reckon? What he did to Jessie was bluffin', was it? Bluff you senseless, he would.'

'Yeah,' said Zac. 'I'm a city-kid, remember?' And to prove it he kicked and stabbed extra high.

This was a big mistake. As he landed, he caught a foot in his folded cape and fell headlong, face downwards.

After that it was just a rugby scrum with Zac playing the part of the ball. Five pairs of heavyweight hands and five sets of heavyweight feet struggled to pummel him all over. 'Say your prayers, city-kid,' snarled Jessie's Number Two.

Zac shut his eyes tight.

Strangely, it was Jessie herself who called them off. 'Hold it!' she choked. 'Just hold it, will you! What was that thing he tripped over? Give it 'ere.'

Still groggy, but very much back in charge, she clambered to her feet. When she shook out the waterproof and held it up to herself, it looked no bigger than a smock. 'This isn't Smokey's,' she scowled. 'It's made to fit this kid. So where did he get it?'

'Where d'you think?' Zac choked. 'Smokey Joe gave it to me himself – to keep off dogs and suchlike. I've been wearing it all day.'

'You've been with Smokey all day?'

'Helpin'.' He felt so battered he could hardly get the word out.

Jessie was sucking her gold tooth again. Now, though, her slurps didn't sound sinister at all – more bewildered, if anything. 'Look, kid,' she said at last 'maybe there's been a mistake. We thought you'd stolen Smokey Joe's bike.'

'Stolen it? Who'd want to steal a bike like that?'

'Some sort of city-kid scam, we reckoned. We thought we were protectin' Smokey's property, see? Never crossed our minds you were helpin' him. You okay, are you?'

'No thanks to you lot,' Zac sniffed.

She looked relieved. 'Gettin' old, Smokey is. He could do with an extra pair of hands now and again. We've known that for donkey's years. But when it came to choosin' his helper . . . well, we expected he'd go for one of us.'

Zac could hear the disappointment in her voice. He could see it, too, in the way she was standing

– in the way every one of them was standing – awkward and shame-faced in the gathering dusk. Across the green, where thatched roofs and chimneypots were picked out against the last brightness of the sky, a lamp flicked on in an upstairs window.

Carefully, Zac brushed the grass from his jeans. 'How could he choose one of you?' he asked. 'You're *all* friends of Smokey, aren't you? That would be favouritism. So he was bound to go for a stranger, right?'

'You reckon?' Jessie said.

'So he told me.'

'Smokey Joe did? He told you that?'

'Obvious, isn't it?'

'Yeah,' said Jessie, perking up.

By the time Zac had slipped the waterproof over his head again and straightened up the bike, most of them were smiling.

Zac made sure he smiled back.

Okay, so he'd bent the truth a little. He'd bet a million quid to a milkbottle top Smokey Joe would have done the same.

Vigil

Much later, when Zac told Smokey Joe what had happened, the old man beamed with delight. 'You catch on fast, son, no doubt about that. Couldn't have treated young Jessie better myself. She's a kid who means well . . . but a tad heavy-handed, you might say.'

'Yeah,' Zac agreed. 'You might.'

He huddled a little closer to the fire.

How late was it, he wondered?

Above them, the sky was already dusty with stars and they were still miles from the vicarage. Would the Reverend and Mrs Reverend wait up for him or just leave the door on the latch so he could creep upstairs without waking them? 'Will we be going back soon?' he asked.

'Back?' said Smokey Joe.

'Home,' said Zac. 'To sleep.'

'What's to stop us dossin' down here, son?'

'Here?'

'Anything wrong with here?'

'Nothing,' said Zac. 'Nothing at all. Won't they be expecting us, though? Their Holinesses, I mean?'

Smokey Joe shook his head. 'Not till tomorrow, they won't. After supper at the earliest, I told 'em. That was assumin' you took to the trade, son – which you have done, by my way of thinkin'. Took to it like a frog to a lily-pad, in fact. O' course, you've still got the actual grinding to come . . .'

'Have I?'

'Fancy makin' the sparks fly, do you?'

Zac's tongue was too heavy to move all of a sudden.

Smokey Joe chuckled. 'Thought so. Got your eyes on the goggles, I 'spect. Most kids take a shine to these goggles.'

'And tomorrow you'll let me wear them?'

'Wouldn't be surprised. Bit of practice after the sun comes up and you'll soon find your touch. From then on, it'll be the real thing for you.'

'The real thing . . .' Zac whispered. He felt dizzy with excitement.

How could he possibly sleep with the real thing only hours away?

ZAC CARBORUNDUM EST.

In a daze, he helped Smokey Joe bury what was left of their late night supper, then hollow out the shape of two beds between the roots of the trees. From the box on the bike, the old man fetched a pair of sleeping bags. 'Lay out your waterproof underneath,' he advised. 'Keeps the damp from strikin' up. Should be comfy enough for one night – especially if I toss a log or two on the fire to keep it goin'. Ever slept in the open before?'

'Never.'

'Better than indoors,' Smokey said. 'Well, better than some indoors at any rate.'

Also better than some outdoors, Zac wanted to add, if outdoors meant a draughty shop entrance or a dank, smelly underpass in the city centre. Did Smokey Joe know about such places?

Anyway, Zac did.

But this place was somewhere else. Here the darkness felt rich with things growing, with nocturnal creatures on the prowl, with a sense of the earth turning as you lay back and stared at the night.

Of course, it was spooky too. For a start it left your brain so clear you couldn't stop random thoughts popping in . . . thoughts you'd prefer to shut out, perhaps. Slyly, unexpectedly, like a

note pushed under a door, or a page falling open in a book, they took you over.

Zac shut his eyes as tight as he could but somehow this only made the images sharper still.

He saw himself curled up in Jeff's big, baggy armchair as he read and read and read . . . concentrating so fiercely it was sometimes hard to tell if he were looking at the words or the words were looking at him.

He heard Elsa's whoop of delight whenever he solved one of her maths problems — loud enough to greet a winning goal at Wembley let alone the answer to a sum.

He remembered the fuss they always made of him when he brought home his latest glowing school report.

They'd been playing it up a bit, obviously. He wasn't so blind he missed that. Partly they were out to encourage him, he realised, and partly to let the other kids know — the bouncy, rough-and-tumble kids who were into Rock and Sport and Video-Games — that it was okay to be book-ish as well. 'Honestly, there's reading stuff everywhere you look in this place,' newcomers always said. 'Stacks and stacks of it! It's like living in a library.'

'Anything the matter with that?' Jeff would ask.

'Course not,' they'd reply.

After all, he was Judo Jeff — the only Housefather they'd ever met who'd won a black belt.

So they left Zac alone with his books and his writing-pads. They hardly teased him at all for being such a boffin. In a way, they became quite proud of him. 'Shush!' they'd hiss outside Jeff's room. 'Zac's in there studying for his exam.'

Which is what Zac had done, day after day, week after week, month after month — practically morning, noon and night towards the end — 'til it wasn't much of a surprise at all, quite frankly, when the exam itself turned out to be a bit of a doddle.

A doddle, yes.

He'd even spent the last ten minutes the way Elsa recommended, reading through what he'd written to correct any careless errors. There weren't any, he was sure of that.

Pity, then, about the interview afterwards . . .

Even now, in his sleeping bag, Zac felt queasy all over again as the scene re-played itself in his head: two posh-looking gents in suits and a lady with clicky teeth who never stopped smiling. They'd been so *nice* to him, hadn't they? They'd let him talk himself hoarse while they scribbled their notes at a long, bench-like table cluttered with papers. Then, as they showed him out of the room, one of them had said, 'It's been a pleasure to meet you, Isaac.'

Instantly, he'd known something was wrong.

A few days later, in an envelope with a fancy crest, the letter had arrived. Zac could quote it word-for-word:

Dear Mr Mason and Ms Tilbury

Thank you so much for sending Isaac Spenser to take our entrance tests. He performed very well indeed on the written papers. Please pass on our warmest congratulations. However, as you know, we have many more applicants each year than we can possibly accept and very much regret that we are unable to offer him a place at the College for next September.

We wish you and Isaac well, though, in finding the right secondary school for him.

Yours sincerely
Reginald Atkinson
Admissions Officer

That's all there was.

End of story.

Zac Spenser, ex-boffin.

Of course, he was expected to take this disappointment in his stride. He was supposed to ignore all the nudges and knowing looks – all the whispering behind his back that the school had turned him down because of his colour, or because he was poor, or because he'd spent most of his life in a children's home.

Such talk wasn't worth his attention according to Jeff and Elsa.

They'd spent hours trying to convince him they were right. Or was it to convince themselves? In some ways, they'd seemed just as upset as he was . . . except with them it had come out as weariness and with him as anger.

He remembered the anger.

He'd made a pile of it, hadn't he – stone by stone and brick by brick – in a handy industrial-size wheelbarrow? Then, on a night very much like this one, he'd pushed it round the outside of the building, window by window, laughing crazily at every direct hit he'd scored.

No, not the College building. He'd been much too furious for that. It was the Children's Home he'd attacked.

When they finally came out to stop him, both with topcoats over their nightclothes, Elsa's face had been blank and tight-lipped in the moonlight as she stared at the shards of glass, while Jeff, he could have sworn, had tears in his eyes.

Zac squirmed at the memory.

Straight away he froze as he heard Smokey Joe heave himself up on an elbow. 'Somethin' botherin' you, son?' he yawned.

'Just . . . just a twig, I think,' said Zac. 'It jabbed me in the back as I turned over.'

'Serve you right,' Smokey said. 'Nobody made that bed of yours except yourself.'

Zac stayed as quiet and still as he could after that 'til the weazy in-and-out of the old man's breathing had hardened into a snore.

Not like Zac's. Zac had never felt less like sleeping.

As the logs crumbled slowly to ashes and the shadows crept closer and closer, voices he'd rather not hear floated out of the dark and into his brain one after the other. Even the old lady at the castle came back to torment him with her questions about Smokey Joe. 'Where d'you expect it to get you, boy?' she asked over and over again. 'What's in it for you?'

'Only the goggles,' he told her. 'That's all I'm after, Mrs Reeve. Through those goggles the world will look different.'

'But will it *be* different, boy?'

'I don't know.'

Was it not knowing that kept him awake?

Or just the reminder of shattering glass?

Whichever it was, lying there on the forest floor with much more than the jab of a twig-or-two to bother him, Zac watched the sky slowly cloud over star by star.

Rain on the Parade

At last morning came.

All through washing, eating and striking camp, Zac barely spoke. 'Cat got your tongue, young feller?' Smokey Joe asked.

'Squirrel,' said Zac.

'Red one or grey one?'

'Red . . . red as the sun behind those trees.'

Smokey looked up from the toolbox and scowled at the horizon. 'Shepherd's warnin', that is,' he remarked.

'Is it going to rain?'

'Cats and dogs, son – also squirrels, I shouldn't wonder. But not for hours yet. Want to practise on the stone for a bit before the weather breaks?'

'Yeah,' Zac said.

'Better wear this pair o' mittens, then. My knobbly old hands got spark-proof long ago but yours will be soft as a baby's botty.'

'Thanks.'

'Don't mention it,' said the old man. 'Oh, and we mustn't forget these, must we.' Grinning, he handed over the goggles.

Zac stared at them, awestruck.

He wanted to admire the way their metal frames caught what little daylight there was. He wanted to test the elastic to make sure they wouldn't flop down around his shoulders. He wanted to give them a quick spit-and-polish for luck . . . anything, that is, except actually put them on.

But already the grindstone was buzzing. 'Here,' said Smokey Joe briskly, 'this axe will get you started.'

'Okay,' Zac swallowed. He pulled the goggles over his face.

At once the world went golden: golden close up, golden far off and golden in-between – as if a mad King Midas had been out on a tickling spree. 'Keep your eyes set on the carborundum,' ordered Smokey Joe. 'Feel the edge of the blade through your fingertips. Let the stone kiss it not gnash it.'

'Like this?' Zac asked.

'Steady now, son. Take it very, very steady. A fine blade needs a firm hand and no messin'.'

Zac took it as steadily as he could.

Metal nudged against metal . . .

A scatter of pinprick light on his gloves and goggles . . .

Both hands firm and no messin'.

That's how the morning ticked by. Zac was discovering for himself (which was the only way to do it) how a shift of grip or angle or pressure could cope with any edge there was.

The first drops of fat, Spring rain didn't slow him down for a moment. 'Umbrella!' was all he said.

Smokey Joe raised it without a word.

They'd never worked so hard in their lives.

Eventually, even Zac was satisfied. He stepped back from the bike. 'Finished,' he said wearily.

'No oilstone, then?' said Smokey Joe. 'No

whetstone?'

'Didn't I learn those yesterday?'

'Yesterday was practice, son. Today it's unfinished business. Small jobs or big jobs . . .'

'. . . treat 'em both with respect,' Zac nodded. Already he was reaching for the toolbox.

This time he kept going till the sun had reached its peak for the day – not that anyone could tell behind the brooding, heavy-duty cloud. 'It's darker than it was at dawn,' Zac grumbled as they left the clearing.

'Warmer, though,' said Smokey Joe. The old man dabbed at his forehead with a hanky the size of a hand towel. Zac saw how bright his eyes were.

'Are you okay?' he asked.

'Fair to middlin', I suppose.'

'We don't have to go to the parade, if you don't want to, Smokey Joe. You look a bit feverish . . .'

'And you sound a bit doctor-ish,' the old man snapped.

There was no answer to that.

Zac concentrated on wheeling the bike.

Even this was much easier now as if the machine had shrunk overnight or somehow he'd managed to grow. 'I can actually balance the thing!' he exclaimed.

'And shift it faster, son.'

This was true, too. He had to slow down every so often to let Smokey Joe catch up.

They reached the village sooner than he expected. It looked down on the castle's main gate 'like a porter's lodge that's got a bit above itself' in Smokey Joe's words. Zac saw what he meant. A square, a criss-cross of streets and three parts open country to one part castle wall was the best anyone could say for it. He'd visited shopping precincts that were more impressive.

But not more congested.

Despite the rain, which glistened on every surface, the square was a hugger-mugger mass of fidgeting, gossiping people – most of them friends of Smokey Joe, apparently. As the old man shuffled by, hands were offered for shaking and cheeks to be kissed. 'Hi, Smokey! Where have you been?'

'Got a tricky item for you, old chap . . .'

'Heavens, Joe, you're more gigantic than ever! Still got those wonderful goggles, I see.'

Zac was astonished. 'Does everyone who lives in the country know everyone else?' he asked.

'Sometimes it feels that way, son. Look, why don't you wriggle down to the front – with all these rainhats and umbrellas in the way, you'll miss everythin' this far back. We can meet up again afterwards.'

'Good idea,' said Zac.

For a city-kid, especially one who was used to football crowds on a Saturday afternoon, it was easy-peasy.

In no time at all, he'd wormed his way forwards and was peering over a makeshift barrier into a space the size and shape of a circus-ring. Opposite, dripping with banners, were the tight-shut gates of the castle. He glanced at the girl in a duffle-coat standing next to him. 'Does the parade come through there?' he pointed.

'And goes out,' she said.

'A procession up to the castle, right?'

'Like every year, yes.' She was peering at him curiously. 'Is that some kind of Smokey Joe outfit?' she asked. 'Where's it come from?'

'Hollywood,' said Zac.

'What?'

'It's from SMOKEY JOE: THE MOVIE. We've just begun shooting on location.'

'And you're playing Smokey Joe?'

'Why not?'

'Because you're – '

'Yes?'

' – just a kid,' she finished lamely.

'That's what I'm meant to be,' said Zac. 'I'm only the young Smokey Joe, you see. Someone else plays him as a grown-up.'

'Oh yeah? And who would that be?'

'Whoopie Goldberg.'

They were still giggling, Zac as much as the girl, when the gates swung open to an ear-splitting fanfare of trumpets. 'It's the village band!' she exclaimed. 'Look, there's my cousin.'

They were kids like themselves, mostly, playing brass and drums and glockenspiel. Their uniforms were so soggy with rain every one seemed to be shrinking on its wearer as you watched. 'What do you think?' the girl asked.

'Ace,' said Zac.

To tell the truth, he was disappointed. Wasn't it all a bit . . . well, bumpkin-ish? It wasn't a

patch on last Easter's trip with Elsa to see the Lord Mayor's Show.

That is, it wasn't till Sir Lancelot, Sir Gawain and Sir Bedevere rode through the archway.

Zac heard himself gasp.

From the dazzle of their shields and surcoats to the way each horse – no, each stallion – swished spray from its mane and tail, all three of them were magnificent. As they trotted forward, the rain seemed to wrap their armour in a ghostly, metallic haze like the last lingerings of another world.

No wonder the band stood to attention and the crowd held its breath.

In the pin-drop silence of the square, Zac could count every jingle of harness, every clatter of iron-shod feet on the cobbles. 'Brilliant,' he

whispered. 'Truly brilliant.' He wanted to drop on one knee to be knighted.

Slowly, their mounts at a canter now and their plumes and accoutrements marvellously bedraggled, the horsemen made their circuit of the ring – though not a complete circuit. Directly in front of Zac, they pulled up line-abreast in a skitter of hooves. Three vizors flipped open in unison. 'Hi there, kid,' said Sir Bedevere. 'How's tricks?'

'Fine,' Zac croaked.

'Good to hear that . . .' Sir Bedevere bent forward, over the barrier, and lowered his voice. 'Any second thoughts about that job of ours?' he asked. 'There's still a vacancy, you know – not a life's work, exactly, but a bit of fun for the holiday.'

'We really need you, Zac,' said Sir Lancelot.

'Especially him,' Sir Gawain added.

Zac caught the smiles on their faces and how their words echoed slightly inside their helmets. He shook his head in dismay. 'I'd love to help you, I really would, it's just that . . .'

'Oilstones and whetstones, huh?'

Zac nodded.

Sir Bedevere grinned down at him. 'That's what I reckoned you'd say. This pair of nerds bet me you'd have changed your mind by now.

They'll be buying me beer for the rest of the week, thanks to you. Good on you, Zac. Fancy a Lap of Honour?'

'A Lap of Honour – for me?'

'Why not?' said Sir Bedevere. 'We city-folk must stick together.'

Before Zac could move, a sword-arm was circling his waist like a stainless-steel lifebelt. With one swift heave, he was up in the saddle. 'Giddy-up!' someone said.

Maybe it was Zac himself . . .

Later, of course, the ride seemed to be over in the blink of an eye. At the time it was more like slow motion – every bump up and down, every twitch of the reins, every creak of leather or clank of armour stored carefully away in Zac's memory. For him, and for every kid there who was bursting to be him (which meant every kid in the square), the waving and cheering and

clapping lasted a lifetime.

When he was hoisted back over the barrier as neatly as if they'd rehearsed it a hundred times, Zac was almost too dazed to speak. 'Thanks,' he stammered. 'Thanks a lot.'

'Our pleasure, young squire. Stay lucky, now.'

'You too,' said Zac. And he watched them clatter splashily away.

The girl in the duffle-coat was stunned. 'Are they in the movie as well?' she gasped.

'Just friends of mine,' Zac said.

'Cool.' She nodded understandingly as if this were no more than she expected from a colleague of Whoopie Goldberg's. 'I'd better be off,' she said. 'My Mum and Dad have booked seats up at the tournament. They'll kill me if I get left behind. See you, then.'

'See you,' said Zac.

Standing there, though, with the square emptying around him and everyone eager to pat him on the back as they passed, he couldn't help wondering if he'd got it right. 'Maybe I was daft to say no,' he groaned. 'Maybe I should have been their technical adviser.'

'You think so?' said Smokey Joe.

Zac turned round at once. When he saw how the old man looked, he didn't think so at all.

Zac Carborundum Est

'It's just a touch of the collywobbles,' growled Smokey Joe. 'Take no notice and it'll cure itself. So let's keep our minds on the job, young-feller-me-lad, and that's an order.'

'Job?' said Zac. 'What job?'

'Today's job,' Smokey Joe answered. 'It's the last one on my rota as it happens. And it's not for puttin' off. That's if you're still willin' to give me a hand, o'course.' His gaze would have been fierce without the deadness in his eyes. There was nothing bright about them now. They looked as if they hadn't been shut for a thousand years.

Zac licked his lips. 'Suppose I've had enough,' he said. 'Suppose I don't want to help you any more.'

The old man shrugged. 'Your privilege, son.'

'You'll go without me, you mean? On your own? Even with . . . with a touch of the

75

collywobbles?'

A snort was all the answer he got.

So Zac just stood there.

What else could he do? How could he possibly stop Smokey Joe's slow, steady plod out of the village? Anyway, wasn't it better to give up now than be stuck in some lonely spot with a sick old man — and no chance at all of fetching an ambulance? Surely this was a situation for grown-ups.

The trouble was . . . there weren't any grown-ups about.

Zac hunched his shoulders and swore under his breath. 'You're such a pigheaded old git,' he snarled. 'The last job on the rota can't be *that* important.' Then he hurried after Smokey Joe.

To his surprise, their route took them deeper and deeper into the woods. The clearing where they'd camped last night had been left behind long ago and so had any proper path through the trees. 'Where *is* this job?' he demanded.

'Tricky to find, son. And every year it gets trickier. Don't let it worry you. I've never missed it yet.'

'So it's a regular job, is it?'

'Regular as Christmas or Midsummer's Day. You won't find it in anyone's diary, though.'

'Except yours,' said Zac.

'Not even in mine. Never written anythin' down in my life, to tell the truth. No reason to when it's all up here in the brain.'

'And all down there in the fingertips,' Zac added.

'Yours, too.'

'Right,' said Zac. Actually, it was his own fingertips he'd meant.

After this, forcing a way through the undergrowth took most of their attention. Already the trees overhead had meshed into a sort of roof. For all Zac knew, the rain could be over — impossible to tell in woodlands so dense he felt he was only a footstep away from a wolf

or a troll or a Hobbit. 'Let's hope it's a Hobbit,' he gulped.

'Do what?' asked Smokey Joe.

'Nothing,' said Zac. 'Er . . . is it much further?'

'Nearly there, I reckon.'

Zac sighed. That's what grown-ups always said. Probably they still had a million wolf-steps or troll-steps or Hobbit-steps to go.

And what about witches?

Wasn't this just the right situation for a house made of gingerbread?

Get a life, he told himself. Are you losing your grip, Zac? Think of street lamps and tower blocks and twenty-four-hour supermarkets . . . fill your mind with something *city-ish* as an antidote.

Suddenly, he saw a glimmering between the trees.

Water, was it?

Yes, water – an eerie-looking stretch of it, gun-metal grey, which seemed to widen and deepen as the trees thinned away. Smokey Joe brought the bike to a halt at the water's edge. He mopped his face with his handkerchief. 'Thought we'd never get here,' he said.

'You mean this is it?'

'Pretty nearly, son. Over there is where we're

due to do the job.'

'Over *there*?' said Zac in dismay. He followed the line of the old man's gaze to the far side of the lake where it was hard to separate high-level forest from low-level cloud. 'How are we supposed to get across?' he asked.

'Usin' this.' Carefully, as if it were a secret he would have preferred to keep, Smokey Joe lifted back a spray of evergreen leaves.

Underneath, in the shallows, was a rowing boat.

Zac eyed it suspiciously. Surely something so frail and weather-worn would never remain afloat with a bike, a boy and a huge old man on board. Luckily, Smokey Joe seemed to agree. 'The bike must be left behind,' he said. 'Untie that toolbox, son. Shift it into the boat along with the battery and the rest of the gear. Make sure you stow it where it'll stay dry.'

Splashing knee-deep through the icy water, Zac did as he was told.

The boat sank lower with the extra weight.

Smokey Joe frowned. 'I thought as much. Zac, that there boat's become a liability. Got drownin' written all over it – for someone my size at any rate. This job is down to you, I reckon.'

'Down to *me*?'

'No need to panic, son. Been trained, haven't you? Besides, the way sound carries over water, you'll pick up every word I say. Just keep on rowin' till I tell you to stop. I'll talk you through the job stage by stage . . . from right here.'

'Here?' said Zac. 'You're staying here?'

'In this very spot. The question is . . . d'you reckon you can cope on your own?'

It was hard to miss the whiteness of the old man's knuckles as he gripped the bike's crossbar – or his weight on the bike itself. So what choice did Zac have? 'No problem,' he said thickly.

'Good,' said Smokey Joe. He took a step backwards as if his relief at Zac's reply had knocked him off kilter. 'Good,' he said again.

For a city-kid, Zac handled the boat rather well. True, his strokes were a bit choppy at first but by the time he was rowing straight (two pulls with his left hand to one with his right), his wake over the surface was almost respectable. The figure of Smokey Joe, faintly ogre-like under the trees, grew smaller and smaller. 'Look!' Zac paused to shout. 'I'm halfway across already.'

'Better stop rowin', then,' Smokey Joe shouted back.

'Stop rowing?' Zac's surprise almost lost him an oar.

He had water all round him. The sky was watery, too, now the rain had stopped. Even the sun, visible at last in the treetops to the west, had a pale, washed-out look.

'Let yourself drift,' called Smokey Joe.

'Drift?' Zac repeated.

'You heard me.' However hard he was to see on the shadowy lakeside, Smokey Joe's words were clear enough.

Again, Zac did as he was told.

At once there were further instructions. 'Start up the grindstone. Lay out all the stuff beside you where it's easy to reach. This is no job for a fumblefist.'

'Like you showed me, Smokey Joe?'

'Exactly like that.'

Zac checked it item-by-item while the

grindstone picked up speed. Yes, everything was in order.

'Ready?' Smokey asked.

'Ready,' said Zac.

'Now's the time to concentrate, then. Keep your mind on what you're doin' . . . and lower those goggles.'

Straight away, the day was golden again – or as much of it as Zac could vouch for with his eyes focused on a carborundum stone, plus fanbelt attachment, linked to a twelve-volt car battery.

So the fuss of water to starboard was something he heard rather than saw . . . along with a clatter of heavy metal as the last job on Smokey Joe's rota landed in the bows of the ramshackle boat.

What else could it be but a sword?

As he held it across his lap, Zac had all the proof he needed that every slender, dripping inch was fit only for a king. 'MERLIN ME FECIT,' he read on the blade. 'That must be Latin for MERLIN MADE ME.' He sat there, too astonished to move.

But Smokey Joe had other ideas. 'Feel the edge of the blade through your fingertips,' he prompted. 'Let the stone kiss it not gnash it.'

Zac counted slowly to ten.

Never, never rush yourself, right? Small jobs or big jobs — treat 'em both with respect.

He took the sword in both hands: blue-ish steel on blackish stone. Instantly, as if the lake were brimful of fireworks and the boat had sprung a leak, he was smothered in sparks. These were sparks with a difference, though, like the splitting of star-shaped atoms or the shaping of atom-split stars.

At just the right moment — he could *tell* it was just the right moment — he switched to the oilstone and whetstone. So fine, so keen was his honing, he knew even before he'd finished that the owner of such a sword could have sliced a human hair from tip to follicle, then sliced it again . . . and again. 'ZAC CARBORUNDUM EST,' he breathed.

'What next, son?' asked Smokey Joe.

'This,' Zac answered. He didn't dare think twice about it.

Ignoring the pitch and toss of the boat, he whirled the sword over his head — faster and faster — till its sharpness sang in the air.

At last he let go.

For as long as a heart can skip a beat (or so it seemed to Zac) the whole world hung in the balance. Finally, from somewhere to starboard, he heard the slap of a hilt in a hand — definitely a hand – and the hiss of a perfect blade as it slid underwater.

Zac might have floated there forever in the sudden stillness – except he had Smokey Joe to look after. 'Good work, son,' the old man was saying. 'Reckon we've got another satisfied customer.'

'Reckon we have,' said Zac. He pushed the goggles high on his forehead to make the world normal again. Then he reached for the oars. 'Now it's your turn, Smokey Joe.'

'My turn?'

'Let's get these collywobbles looked at.'

This time the old knife-grinder didn't argue.

Envoi

Somehow, without even trying, Smokey Joe had taken the Hospital over. His get-well-soon cards covered every wall in the ward and the flowers he'd been sent spilled right along the corridor and out into the front lobby. People had to walk round them during visiting hours.

The boneshaker had its place, too. There it was, back in full working order, propped between the door and the bedside table. 'Told 'em I had to keep my eyes on it right round the clock on account of the other knife-grinders,' he explained. 'Nick it as soon as look at it, they would.'

'What other knife-grinders?' Zac asked. 'You're the only one that's left round here, aren't you?'

'Who me?' said Smokey Joe. His eyes widened innocently as if the local highways and byways were crawling with hotshot competition.

He reached for a grape. 'Sure you won't have one?' he offered.

'No thanks.'

'They're juicy – brought in by his Holiness.'

'I know,' said Zac. 'I helped him choose them, didn't I? I told you that.'

'So you did, son.' Smokey sank back on the pillows. Even with his cape replaced by pyjamas (the largest set the hospital had in stock) he made the bed seem half-size. Both his feet spilled out of the end of it, for instance, as if they'd come up for air.

He wouldn't be here much longer, Zac realised, now they'd sorted him out.

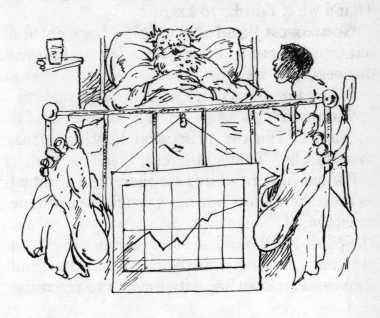

Smokey lifted an eyebrow. 'Pills,' he said. 'That's what they've foisted on me – pills I'll be poppin' for the rest of my life. Should be enough to keep me goin', they say, with a bit of extra help now and again from Jessie and her mates.'

'Fine,' said Zac. 'That's fine, Smokey Joe.'

'Is it, son?' There was a small avalanche of bedclothes as Smokey Joe sat up. 'Doesn't strike me as fine,' he complained. 'Doesn't strike me as the least bit fine when there's a kid I've specially trained wastin' his time and talent up there in some city classroom day after day. O' course, I'm no scholar – never pretended to be – but what's the point of all this school stuff? That's what I'd like to know.'

'So would I,' said Zac. 'Going back to find out *is* the point in a way. It's unfinished business, you see.'

'You sure about that?'

'I am, yes.'

'Ah . . .' The old man scratched his beard, thoughtfully. 'That's different, then,' he said.

For a while they both sat there, not wanting to drop the subject but not wanting to continue it either. Through the window, out in the Hospital grounds, Zac saw distinct signs of growing – blossom, mostly, but also catkins and stickybuds. Even a city-kid can recognise catkins and stickybuds. He wanted to smell them and touch them to make sure they were real. No wonder Smokey Joe hated indoors.

In which case, why was the old man smiling all of a sudden?

He bent forward to tap Zac on the knee. The look on his face was the craftiest Zac had ever seen. 'How about takin' a *regular* holiday down in the country?' he suggested. 'About this time o' year, I mean – to keep yourself up to scratch with the sharpenin', like?'

'That would be *brilliant* . . .'

'You could stay with the Reverends, son. Or even up at the castle if you can stomach that ol' trout with the carvin'-knives. It doesn't matter where, does it, so long as the two of us can get together for a Special Spring rota!'

Zac felt the hair on his scalp prickle. 'Can you fix it, Smokey Joe?' he whispered. 'Jeff and Elsa will agree, I bet. They're always telling me I need more fresh air and exercise. But how about this end? Can you really, really fix it?'

'Nothin' easier,' the old man said. He stretched out a hand even bigger than Jessie's and brushed an imaginary speck of dust from the boneshaker's front wheel. 'In fact,' he went on, 'consider it fixed already, young feller. What you've got to remember is . . .' He paused to let

Zac finish off.

'You're pretty famous in these parts?'

'Exactly,' said Smokey Joe.

Also by Chris Powling

Ziggy and the Ice Ogre

In Fountain City there were fountains simply everywhere and if you stuck your hand under the spray you soon had a helping of the best ice-cream you've ever tasted. Then one day quite suddenly it stopped. No one had ever thought where it came from, but Ziggy knew and she set off to find the Ice Ogre at once.

Chris Powling

The Phantom Carwash

Lenny dreams of getting a rear carwash for Christmas, but he knows he'll have to do without. He thinks his gran is mad when she tells him to write to Santa Claus – but when something strange turns up on the wasteground near his home, he begins to wonder if she was right after all.

Gillian Cross

The Crazy Shoe Shuffle

It is Lee's worst day ever! First, sour Mr Merton confiscates his football. Secondly, Lee makes sweet Miss Cherry cross. Thirdly, bossy Mrs Puddock, the headmistress, forces him to eat his disgusting school dinner.

On top of it all, he finds himself sorting out the shoe mountain in the cloakroom for Miss Cherry and gets on the wrong side of Mr Merton and Mrs Puddock again!

But on the way home he meets a strange old woman and suddenly the boot is on the other foot. The three teachers find themselves in the children's shoes and they're right out of step with everyone else. Only Lee knows what's happened – and he'll have to keep on his toes if he wants to save them from falling flat on their faces . . .

"eight-year-olds upwards . . . will love The Crazy Shoe Shuffle, a fast-moving school comedy . . ."
Sunday Telegraph

GILLIAN CROSS IS WINNER OF THE **WHITBREAD AWARD, THE SMARTIES GRAND PRIX** AND **THE CARNEGIE MEDAL.**

Hazel Townson

Charlie the Champion Liar

To keep face after a disappointing birthday, Charlie
Lyle pretends he's been given a video camera. But he
quickly finds that this one small lie draws him into a
whole series of lies when someone suggests he makes
a video of a PE display . . .

A wonderfully funny story by a master storyteller,
whose books have been previously been described
by Stephanie Nettell as "rollicking rough and
tumble fun".

"an amusing story with a bit of a moral . . ."
Junior Bookshelf

A Selected List of Fiction from Mammoth

While every effort is made to keep prices low, it is sometimes necessary to increase prices at short notice. Mandarin Paperbacks reserves the right to show new retail prices on covers which may differ from those previously advertised in the text or elsewhere.

The prices shown below were correct at the time of going to press.

☐	7497 1421 2	**Betsey Biggalow is Here!**	Malorie Blackman	£2.99
☐	7497 0366 0	**Dilly the Dinosaur**	Tony Bradman	£2.99
☐	7497 0137 4	**Flat Stanley**	Jeff Brown	£2.99
☐	7497 0983 9	**The Real Tilly Beany**	Annie Dalton	£2.99
☐	7497 0592 2	**The Peacock Garden**	Anita Desai	£2.99
☐	7497 0054 8	**My Naughty Little Sister**	Dorothy Edwards	£2.99
☐	7497 0723 2	**The Little Prince (colour ed.)**	A. Saint-Exupery	£3.99
☐	7497 0305 9	**Bill's New Frock**	Anne Fine	£2.99
☐	7497 1718 1	**My Grandmother's Stories**	Adèle Geras	£2.99
☐	7497 2395 5	**Flow**	Pippa Goodheart	£2.99
☐	7497 0041 6	**The Quiet Pirate**	Andrew Matthews	£2.99
☐	7497 1930 3	**The Jessame Stories**	Julia Jarman	£2.99
☐	7497 0420 9	**I Don't Want To!**	Bel Mooney	£2.99
☐	7497 1496 4	**Miss Bianca in the Orient**	Margery Sharp	£2.99
☐	7497 0048 3	**Friends and Brothers**	Dick King Smith	£2.99
☐	7497 0795 X	**Owl Who Was Afraid of the Dark**	Jill Tomlinson	£2.99

All these books are available at your bookshop or newsagent, or can be ordered direct from the address below. Just tick the titles you want and fill in the form below.

Cash Sales Department, PO Box 5, Rushden, Northants NN10 6YX.
Fax: 01933 414047 : Phone: 01933 414000.

Please send cheque, payable to 'Reed Book Services Ltd.', or postal order for purchase price quoted and allow the following for postage and packing:

£1.00 for the first book, 50p for the second; **FREE POSTAGE AND PACKING FOR THREE BOOKS OR MORE PER ORDER.**

NAME (Block letters) ....

ADDRESS ....

....

☐ I enclose my remittance for ....

☐ I wish to pay by Access/Visa Card Number

Expiry Date

Signature ....

Please quote our reference: MAND